# The Barefoot Book of
# Dance Stories

To Maddison and Alison, who love to dance – J.Y.

For my girlfriends Sabra and Sharon, who dance to their own beat.
And for their kids, Courtney, Ben, Anthony, Bryce, and, of course, Natalie,
who will maybe now speak to me.
And for Maddison, my research assistant – H. E.Y. S.

For Rima Dapous, never stop dancing! With much love – H. C.

Barefoot Books
124 Walcot Street
Bath BA1 5BG

This book has been printed on 100% acid-free paper
Graphic design by Barefoot Books,
Bath and Judy Linard, London
Colour separation by Grafiscan, Verona
Printed and bound in China by Printplus Ltd

This book was typeset in Typo Upright, Minion,
Pia and Bembo
The illustrations were prepared in watercolour and mixed
media on Arches paper
Hardback ISBN 978-1-84686-218-2

British Cataloguing-in-Publication Data:
a catalogue record for this book is available
from the British Library

1 3 5 7 9 8 6 4 2

# The Barefoot Book of
# Dance Stories

Written by Jane Yolen and Heidi E. Y. Stemple

Illustrated by Helen Cann

Barefoot Books
*Celebrating Art and Story*

# Contents

One of the most famous ballroom dances is the waltz — a gliding, partnered dance in $3/4$ time. It began in Austria in the late 1700s, probably growing out of peasant folk dances, and became very popular during the nineteenth century. Women in long, elegant gowns and men in formal wear would spin around, waltzing together for hours.

So, too, do the princesses in this story by the Brothers Grimm. But, here the shoes are more important. By today's standards, it would take a lot more than one night to wear out a pair of dancing shoes. Early ballroom shoes were made of much lighter materials than they are today — silk or soft leather. They could be worn through pretty quickly if the wearer waltzed all night, as the princesses do in the story.

Noh is one of the oldest forms of storytelling theatre in the world, dating back to court performances in fourteenth-century Japan. Noh actors are traditionally male and wear carved wooden masks for both male and female roles. They cannot change their facial expressions, so instead they use symbolic hand gestures to show what they are feeling.

Throughout the world, there are tales of birds or celestial beings who magically change into maidens. 'Robe of Feathers' is a Japanese version of such a story made into a Noh play. The Japanese people so love the story that there is a statue of Hakuryo carrying the robe at the entrance of Mihonomatsubara Beach, near Mount Fuji — the very spot where the story is supposed to have taken place.

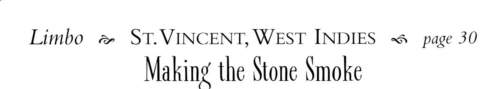

# Making the Stone Smoke

Many people came to the West Indies from Europe and Africa, so dance there includes elements from these cultures as well as from local traditions. One of the most popular dances is the limbo. Plantation owners in the West Indies were less strict about slaves dancing than their counterparts in America, who considered it sinful or dangerous, and even banned drum-playing.

The main character in this story is Anansi from Africa. Portrayed as a boastful, outrageous, scheming, trickster god – often in the form of a spider – he is credited with acts as grand in scale as stealing the sun and creating the earth. Whatever the prize, Anansi is never afraid to go to extraordinary lengths to get what he wants.

# The Shepherd's Flute

Flamenco dancing originated with Spanish gypsies and moved to the ballrooms, cafés, theatres and dance schools of Spain and beyond. Today it is made up of three elements: *cante* (the song), *baile* (the dance) and *guitarra* (the guitar playing). The dance movements are characterised by the *palmada* and *zapateado* – the clapping of the dancers' hands and the stamping of their feet, both of which are usually improvised.

The most important quality a flamenco performer must have is *duende* – a state of intense emotion that is portrayed by the dancer clapping and encouraging exclamations from fellow performers. The power and impact of the flamenco dance is revealed in this tale. Olé!

*Polka* ⁊ CZECH REPUBLIC ⁊ *page 48*

# Dancing with the Birch Fairy

Right in the middle of Europe, sandwiched between Germany and Poland, sit the landlocked countries of Slovakia and the Czech Republic. Prior to 1993, they were one country – Czechoslovakia. It is in this mountainous region that both the story of the birch fairy and the polka originated.

Legend has it that polka was invented in 1834 by a peasant girl named Anna. The original name of the dance, 'pulka', is Czech for 'half-step', which refers to the rapid shift from one foot to the other. A lively dance for two partners, the polka has a hop-step-close-step foot pattern, which the birch fairy performs with Betushka in this story. It is also very addictive – no wonder Betushka forgot all about her work!

*Belly Dancing* ⁊ EGYPT ⁊ *page 60*

# When the Goddess Danced

In ancient Egypt, though there were many types of dance, men and women rarely danced together and no one in the upper classes ever danced in public. The best-known dance from Egypt is belly dancing. However, the ancient form of the dance was not performed as entertainment. One theory runs that it was initially intended as a form of exercise to help women to prepare their muscles for childbirth.

The story of the beautiful Ruditdidit is very old. When an ancient god falls in love with her, he calls on his fellow gods to help her when she goes into labour. She is taught to belly dance by the goddess Isis; this ties in with the theory that belly dancing was also originally a religious dance.

# Tam O'Shanter

In the seventeenth century, dancing was frowned upon by the Church of Scotland. This culminated in a law being passed in 1649 banning men and women from dancing together in public. However, in the Scottish Highlands, where the Church had little power, dancing never went out of fashion. Indeed, it is said of Scottish Reels that while the orchestra sometimes tires of them, the dancers never do.

Here, in the story of farmer Tam – based on a famous narrative poem written in 1790 by Robert Burns – folklore and reeling go hand in hand. The old church ruins and the bridge in the tale are real and stand to this day. In fact, the poet's father lies buried in the kirkyard.

# The Little Bird Who Went Dancing

Oral and musical storytelling traditions are a strong part of Malian culture. Both history and folklore are passed down by storytelling musicians known as 'griots', meaning 'keepers of memories'. Malian society was run on a strict caste system; griots were born into their profession and married within their class. This meant that if a musician was born into another caste, it was not possible to choose to become a griot.

The people of Mali love to dance and will do so at any opportunity, as you will see in this story. In addition to dancing just for fun, there are the celebrated mask dances, performed by the Dogon people of Mali for funeral ceremonies and for a special festival called the 'dama', in which the spirits of the ancestors are worshipped.

# The Twelve Dancing Princesses

Once upon a time, a king had twelve daughters, and each one was more beautiful than the next, the most beautiful being the youngest. They slept all together in one bedroom, their beds side by side. You may think this is odd, but it was a large room.

Every night, the king locked the door on the outside with twelve locks, and then he bolted it with twelve bolts so that the girls could not get out, nor could anyone else get in. He thought in this way to keep his daughters safe. But every morning, when the king came to unlock and unbolt the door, he saw that the princesses' silken shoes were quite worn through, as if the girls had been dancing all night.

The king was puzzled by this. Where could the girls have gone dancing? The room was large, but not big enough for dashing about in. And no one had heard any music.

Neither the king nor his wisest advisors could figure it out. So when he'd exhausted the greatest minds in his kingdom, the king sent out a proclamation to all the kingdoms for a thousand miles around saying that whoever could discover where his daughters went to dance all night could choose one of them for his wife and rule after the king's death.

Well, you would have thought that hundreds of young men would have been eager to try, but they all read the fine print of the proclamation that said whoever came forward and did not discover the secret within three days and three nights would forfeit his life. So there were not as many volunteers as you might guess.

However, there were a few. Within a week, a king's son came forward to try. He was given a huge feast, with seasoned meats and white bread and salads. He drank glass after glass of lovely sweet wine that the princesses themselves poured for him.

After dinner, he was led to a room that adjoined the princesses' chamber, a kind of dressing room. Servants brought in a fine bed for him, with a soft mattress and two featherbeds to keep him warm.

'Mind you observe where the girls go,' said the king. And the prince nodded, trying hard not to yawn in the king's face, for all that feasting had made him sleepy.

'I will watch all night,' he promised. But no sooner had the king closed the door and locked them all in with the twelve locks and bolts than the prince fell fast asleep. When he woke in the morning, it was clear that the twelve princesses had been off dancing, for their shoes had holes worn right through the silken soles.

On the second and third nights, it was just the same, and the poor prince had his head struck off.

After that the executioner was kept busy, for every single young man who tried to solve where the princesses went at night failed and forfeited his life.

Now, it happened that a poor soldier came walking along the road to the king's castle. He was a hero who'd been wounded in one of the many wars and so had been sent home. Wounded or not, he still walked with a soldier's gait: hup and one, hup and two.

Suddenly, he came upon an old woman in the road.

'And where are you going, my good soldier?' she asked.

Luckily for him, he was polite. One should always be polite to mysterious old ladies. Quite often they are filled with magic.

'Grandmother,' he said, 'I hardly know myself.' He gave her a drink of water from his flask and a bit of his hard bread. And then he added, almost as a joke, 'I thought I might try discovering where those twelve beautiful princesses go when they dance their shoes into holes. It would be nice being king.'

'Hah!' said the old woman, 'You are a sensible man, not a whining boy. I like your spirit, courage and honesty. And so I will tell you how to do it. First, you must not drink the wine that the princesses will pour for you. And second, you must pretend to be sound asleep.'

'And third?' asked the soldier, for he'd found that instructions in the army came in threes.

'Third,' she told him, as she gave him a little cloak, 'put on this cloak and you will become invisible. Then you can sneak after the girls and see where they go.'

Well, the soldier was used to danger, and after receiving the cloak and the advice, he knew he was well prepared. So he kissed the old woman on both cheeks and gave her the rest of his water and bread and a bit of cheese he'd been saving for himself. Then he marched — hup and one, hup and two — up to the castle and announced himself.

Just like the others, he was given a grand feast. He pretended to drink the wine, but actually he poured it out into the nearest potted plant.

Then he was brought into the dressing room. As he was about to climb onto the bed, the eldest sister brought him yet another cup of wine. But, being a good soldier, he was prepared and had concealed a sponge under the neck of his nightshirt. He thanked the princess heartily and turned away, pretending to drink the wine down in a single swallow. In reality, he let the wine run down his chin and into the sponge, without ever swallowing a drop.

'Sweet dreams,' the princess said to him.

'And to you,' he answered. Then he lay down and pretended to sleep, snoring so loudly that the princesses all laughed.

The eldest said, 'He is a fine-looking soldier, and all those medals on his chest prove he is a hero. It is too bad that he, too, will have to die. He should have stayed in the army and gone back to war. It would have been safer.'

They all agreed. And then, without further conversation, they opened their wardrobes and got out their prettiest dresses, which were all the colours of the rainbow: pink and rose, yellow and citrine, lavender, blue, aqua and deep heavenly green.

Suddenly, the youngest said, 'Sisters, I feel very strange. Do you not feel it, too? It is as if misfortune is about to befall us.'

The eldest sister put her arms around her. 'Little pretty goose, have you forgotten how many kings' sons have already come here in vain? A soldier will hardly be able to do what they could not.'

So then the girls began to preen and look at themselves in the mirrors, pinching their cheeks to bring out the colour, and laughing, even the youngest. But before they left, they went into the dressing room and stood about the soldier's bed to make sure he was fast asleep. He snored even louder than before.

The eldest then went over to her bed and clapped three times. Immediately, the bed sank into the earth, with steps running all the way down. One after another, the princesses descended the stairs, the eldest going first. The soldier watched everything through slitted eyes, then quietly got up and put on the cloak, becoming invisible. Then, he hurried down, right after the youngest.

Halfway, he accidentally stepped on her dress. Terrified, she cried, 'Sisters, someone is pulling my dress.' But when she turned around, no one was there.

'Little pretty goose,' her eldest sister called back, 'you have only caught your skirt on a nail.'

Then the princesses continued all the way down, and at the bottom of the steps was a broad avenue lined with towering elm trees with leaves made of pure silver.

The soldier thought, 'I must take a token back with me to prove where I have been.' So he broke off a twig from one of the trees, and the sound was as loud as a gunshot.

The youngest princess cried out, 'Sisters, did you hear that crack?'

But the eldest said, 'It is only our escorts firing off their rifles with joy because we got rid of our suitor so quickly.'

All the princesses laughed at that, and the sound was like wind through the silver leaves.

Soon the princesses came to an even broader avenue where the leaves of the trees were all of pure gold, and finally to an avenue where all the leaves were made out of sparkling diamonds. Each time, the soldier broke off a twig, hiding it in the inside pocket of his cloak. Each time he did so, the twig made a dreadful crack. And each time she heard the crack, the youngest princess shook with terror. But her eldest sister continued to maintain that the cracking sounds were just rifle salutes.

At last, the princesses came to a great lake where twelve little boats were anchored. In every boat sat a handsome prince, his hands on the oars, waiting. The princesses each got into a boat, and the soldier sat down by the youngest.

The prince said to the youngest princess, 'How strange. The boat is so much heavier tonight than usual. I shall have to double my strokes to get us across.'

She answered him, 'Everything about tonight is strange.' And she trembled a bit as if with the cold. The soldier had to be very careful not to put his arm around her to keep her warm.

On the far side of the
lake stood a brightly lit castle,
and the soldier could hear the sound of violins
and violas and deep double basses playing waltz after waltz
after waltz. He wanted to tap his foot to the music, but he did not.

Each prince took the arm of his princess, helped her from
the boat and led her into the castle where they danced all night
long in the great ballroom. They did the bouncy Rhinelander polka
that careened over the floor. They performed the enthusiastic
Fingerlestanz where the princesses all stamped their feet and scolded
their partners with shaking fingers. But best of all they did the stately
and graceful waltz, their belled skirts billowing out as they whirled
and twirled across the floor.

The soldier danced, too, hidden from sight by his cloak of
invisibility. When one of the princesses went to drink wine out of a
golden cup set by her side, the soldier drank it up ahead of her. Only
the youngest seemed alarmed at this, but the eldest just said, 'Silly
pretty goose, you are ruining our dance. Be silent.' So she was.

The twelve princesses danced in the magic castle until three o'clock, and their shoes were full of holes. Only then did they stop. The princes rowed them back over the lake, and no one seemed to notice the soldier was there.

'We shall be back tomorrow,' the girls promised the princes. But the soldier had already run up the stairs ahead of them, taken off his cloak of invisibility, and lain down in his bed. By the time the twelve princesses came up into the room, he was snoring loudly.

The princesses were pleased the soldier was still asleep, though once again the eldest said, 'Too bad, soldier, you did not stay at your war where it was safe.'

The next morning, the soldier decided not to say what he'd seen just yet, but to follow the princesses for a second night. Everything happened in the same way, and once again the twelve princesses danced until their shoes were worn through.

On the third night, it was exactly as before, with this one exception: the soldier carried off a golden wine cup from the magic castle as a token, instead of the leaves.

When at last it was time for the soldier to report to the king, he was ready. He took the three twigs and the cup to the throne room and waited until the king was seated with his advisors around him.

'Now tell me, soldier, or lose your head: where do my twelve daughters go at night, with the door locked and bolted?'

The soldier took out the twigs and the cup and told the story of what had happened — about the doctored wine, the three claps, the long steps, the broad avenues and the tall trees. He told the king about the lake and the little boats, with the princes manning the oars. He told him about the castle lit by candlelight and the musicians playing waltz after waltz after waltz. He was fully aware that all the while he spoke, the twelve princesses were behind a door, listening to every word he said.

The king then summoned his daughters around him. 'Does the soldier speak the truth?'

What could they say? All the king would have to do was clap his hands above the eldest daughter's bed and all would be revealed.

'It is true, father,' the eldest princess said. 'We have been under some strange enchantment. And while I do not know who bewitched us, the soldier has broken it forever.'

So the king turned back to the soldier. 'Which princess will you take for a wife?' he asked.

The soldier looked at all twelve princesses, each one more beautiful than the last. Then he said, 'I am no longer young, so give me the eldest.' What he didn't add was that he liked her spirit and her courage and her honesty. That he said privately to her, much later.

So the wedding was celebrated that very day, and the princesses all waltzed across the ballroom, none with more happiness than the eldest princess.

Many years later, when the king had died, the soldier and the eldest princess ruled well, side by side, with spirit, courage and honesty, for a long time after.

# Robe of Feathers

Once a fisherman named Hakuryo took his nets in hand to go fishing near the pine forest of Mio. He had not yet reached the shore when he saw a strange sight. Hanging on the branch of a pine tree was a beautiful robe, made entirely of white feathers.

Hakuryo reached out, took the robe down, and was about to examine it closely, when he realised someone was nearby. Looking up, he saw a beautiful maiden walking towards him.

'Fisherman,' she said, her voice light and liquid, 'give me back my robe.'

He shook his head. 'Your robe, lady? I think it too beautiful for one person. It should be placed with the other great treasures of Japan.'

'Oh, please, fisherman,' she begged him, 'give me the robe. Without it, I cannot fly. If it is put away in a museum, I will never be able to return to my home in the skies. Oh, good fisherman, please give it back.'

Hakuryo still shook his head. It was not that he was hard-hearted; he truly believed the magnificent robe belonged to all the Japanese people.

But the maiden could not stop begging for the return of her robe. 'Would you take my skin, fisherman? Would you steal my wings? Without the robe, I am bound to the earth, even as you are.' She stood before him, wringing her hands.

Hakuryo did not quite understand what it was he held. Was the robe more than just a beautiful object? Could it be magical as well? His heart began to soften.

'Maiden,' he said, bowing to her, 'I will give you back this robe of feathers for a price.'

'I have no money, fisherman. We celestial beings do not barter or trade. We take our living from earth and sky.' She shook her head, and the waterfall of her hair rippled down her back.

'You mistake me, maiden,' Hakuryo said. 'I will give it back to you if you will dance before me.' For he had heard that the celestial beings knew dances that no one on earth had ever seen.

She shook her head again, but there was a smile on her face. 'One dance, fisherman?'

He bowed again, this time very low, knowing that the gods did not reward greed. 'Only one.'

She took a step back and said, 'I will do a dance for you that makes the Palace of the Moon turn around, but. . .' she paused.

Hakuryo glanced up at her. 'But. . . ?'

'But I cannot dance without my feather robe.'

This time it was Hakuryo who shook his head. 'No. Once I give you the robe, you will fly away.'

The maiden stamped her foot. Her face, so beautiful, became almost ugly with anger. 'You mortals may make pledges that you break, but we do no such thing in the heavens. I have said I will dance in return for the robe, and so I shall do.'

Her voice was low, but nevertheless Hakuryo shook with fear and shame. He held out the robe, and the white feathers glistened in the sunlight.

The maiden took the robe and ran her hand down the feathers, as if to calm them. Or like a bird preening itself. Then she took a koto from under the garment, and Hakuryo was astonished, for there had been no instrument there a moment before.

With a quick movement of hand and shoulder, the maiden donned the white feather robe, then struck the strings of the koto, after which it began to

play all by itself. At that, the maiden started to dance, her movements languorous and pure. And as she danced, she sang of her home high up in the moon. The song told of the walls of the palace that were fashioned with a jade axe. It spoke of thirty kings of the moon, fifteen in white robes who ruled when the moon was full and fifteen in black who ruled when the moon waned.

Hakuryo's eyes filled with tears as the sky maiden danced, for he had never seen anything so beautiful.

Then the maiden turned around three times and blessed the islands of Japan, saying: 'Like the pearls of a fine necklace, they shall ever increase in their worth.'

Hakuryo was about to thank her when he saw that the maiden was no longer on the sand. Having fulfilled her promise to give him one dance, she was now walking on the air as if on invisible steps. Higher and higher she went, past the pine trees of Mio, past the Floating Islands, over the mountain of Ashitaka, the high peak of Fuji. Now she no longer looked like a maiden in a white feather robe, but like a white bird, flying upwards to the Palace of the Moon.

The fisherman fell to his knees and wept anew, promising to remember the robe, the maiden and the dance. And he promised to remember this story as well.

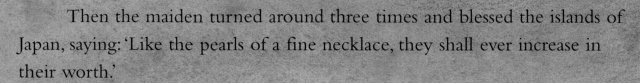

# Making the Stone Smoke

Once upon a time, on the island of St. Vincent, a king had a daughter as beautiful as the sun. And this king, he didn't want anyone to touch her or marry her or get near her for anything in the world, so he put her in a big glass box.

'You can't do that,' said the queen. 'She's a girl, not the crown jewels. She has to be married some day or there won't be anyone to inherit the kingdom.'

The king said, 'I'm not planning to die.'

And the queen said, 'Nevertheless, some day you will. So you'd better start planning for it.'

The king scratched his head and saw the wisdom of his wife's words. But still he hated the idea of anyone marrying his daughter. So he decided to make it very tough for anyone to win her. He sent out a notice all around the island, with a crier who called out, 'Listen up! Listen up!' And when he had everyone's attention, he gave them the king's invitation:

*There is a large stone in the middle of the courtyard. Anyone who can dance this stone into smoke can marry my daughter and get the palace, too.*

The king figured this would be impossible. And for a long while he was right. Many men from the east and west and north and south came, and they danced their shoes to pieces, but they couldn't make that big stone smoke.

'See,' the king told his wife, 'I am giving them a chance.'

'Some chance,' she said. And she went to sit next to the glass box to chat with her girl.

Now far away, Anansi heard about the princess who was as beautiful as the sun, and he gave the matter a great deal of thought. Anansi thinking is not a pretty sight to see. But it usually works out – to Anansi's profit.

After he finished thinking, he went to his tailor. 'Tailor,' said Anansi,

*Make me a red coat with trim all around*
*And special pockets all the way to the ground.*

When the red coat was done, Anansi put it
on and went to the sugar-boiling house and
said to the overseer,

*Put ashes in my pockets, man,*
*And I'll reward you when I can.*

Then he put on his shoes,
the heavy leather ones, and
went off to the king's palace.

The king greeted him
as he had greeted every
other dancer, though
he laughed at little
Anansi behind his
hand. For Anansi
was not only small,
he was ugly.

'Here is my daughter, Anansi,' the king said, pointing to the girl in the glass box. 'There is the stone.' He pointed to the big grey stone. 'Dance it to smoke and she is yours.'

Anansi bowed and went over to the stone that was twice as high and twice as broad as he was. And as he went over, he was already starting to sing and dance:

> *I will set the boxed girl free,*
> *Hidey-ho, that girl's for me.*

His heavy leather shoes began to scuff the ground and he swung his hips and shook himself all over. Quick-quick-slow. Step, rock, close, pause. He did the mambo with great flair. Oh, he was starting to have a really good time.

'What are you singing?' shouted the king.

Anansi sang out even louder:

> *I will set the boxed girl free,*
> *Hidey-ho, that girl's for me.*

Then he turned around, slid his feet about some more, and clapped his hands for the limbo stick. The crowd brought out the stick and held it just inches from the ground. Anansi slid under the limbo stick. As he did so, he secretly began to flap his arms and bang them down hard against the pockets filled with ashes.

*I will set the boxed girl free,*
*Hidey-ho, that girl's for me.*

Four times and four times and four times more he banged against those pockets, slapping his sides and singing loudly as he went under the stick. Then he stood upright and began twirling around. He stomped and he tromped and he shimmied all about. Ashes flew up from the pockets and into the air and all over the courtyard. Grey ashes, like smoke.

The king couldn't see a thing, only the smoky ashes. The queen couldn't see a thing, only the smoky ashes. The beautiful princess behind the glass could see a little better, and she just laughed and laughed, knowing that she would soon be set free.

And still Anansi danced.

'Stop! Stop!' the king cried, afraid that the whole palace would go up in smoke. 'You win. The girl's for you.'

Anansi stopped. He bowed to the king. He bowed to the queen. Then he winked at the princess – and the guards opened the glass box. The girl walked out, free. And if they married, well that's between them, not you or me.

The wire is bended, my story's ended.

# The Shepherd's Flute

Once, near old Granada, there lived a widower with a young son named Pablo. Oh, how the man missed having a wife to make him breakfast and warm his bed. So he married again, but she was a woman who was mean enough to make milk go sour.

Not only was she mean, she thought Pablo was a bother and determined that she would get rid of him. She wanted a son of her own to inherit all that her husband owned.

So she said to her husband, 'It is time for Pablo to earn his keep. Send him up the mountains with a dog to watch the sheep.'

Now Pablo's dog was a clever and watchful sort, named Todo. But there were so many sheep and so many wolves on the mountain, it happened that one lamb got taken.

When they got home the stepmother thwacked Todo with a broom and Pablo with her hand. 'There! And there!' she cried. 'Do you think your father is made of money that he can afford to lose a single lamb?'

Pablo wept, not for himself, and not for Todo, but for the lamb, gone to the wolves. But it did no good. In a month another lamb was gone. And then a third. There were just too many wolves for one boy and one dog to guard against.

Now one awful day in the autumn, the wind blew up, snow fell down, and all the silly sheep scattered. Try as they might, Pablo and his dog could only find half a dozen of them.

'She will not just thwack us this time,' he told Todo miserably, 'but will likely kill us.' He put his head in his hands and began to weep.

Todo barked, a short, sharp sound, and Pablo looked up. There, before him on the mountain, stood an old peasant woman, a black kerchief around her shoulders. She stared at Pablo with sharp, dark eyes. 'I smell trouble,' she said, lifting her head as if sniffing the wind.

Pablo stood and bowed his head. She may have looked like a peasant woman, but no peasant women ever came up into the mountains, and Pablo was the kind of boy who knew the old stories. 'I have lost my sheep, señora,' he said, and bowed his head to her again.

She smiled at him, her teeth white and shining. And that was when Pablo knew for certain that she was no ordinary old woman, for there were no peasants with teeth like that.

'You are a good boy, Pablo,' the woman said. 'I have been keeping my eye on you.' She put her hand into the bosom of her dress and drew out a silver flute. At the end of the flute were two tiny carved pomegranate flowers. 'So here is a gift for you.' She handed him the flute and then, in an instant, was gone.

Eagerly, he held the flute to his mouth, pursed his lips and began to play. A lovely, lilting song, like the call of the thrush, came trembling out of the flute. And that was odd indeed because he'd never played a note before.

Todo barked and began
to dance the flamenco on his hind legs,
and behind him came all the lost sheep,
dancing the bolero in a line: rams and ewes and even lambs.

It was so funny, Pablo took the flute from his lips and bent over in laughter.

The minute the music stopped, the dog was back on all fours barking at the sheep, and the sheep began to crop the grass as if they'd never been dancing.

Well, from that day on, Pablo and his dog and sheep enjoyed their time in the mountain pasture. But they danced so much, the sheep did not gain weight. In fact, they grew slim and muscular.

So when Pablo brought them home each evening, his stepmother was furious. She screamed and yelled at him. She thwacked and whacked both boy and dog until they were black and blue. Pablo's father did not stop her, but went out onto the terrace to smoke his pipe. There he complained to all the neighbours about what a difficult son he had.

Meanwhile, the stepmother had picked up the great copper pot, hard a-boil with beans for supper. She was about to throw it at the dog, when Pablo took out his silver flute and began to play.

In the cottage, the notes of the flute
echoed from the walls, sounding like a
hundred thrushes were singing all together.
Still holding the pot, the stepmother began to
dance. She beat on the copper pot as if it were
a drum, flung her legs about, and went round
and round the room. Oh, how she danced, the
soup splashing out on her hands and arms and
even on her feet. She howled with pain, but
she could not stop dancing.

In rushed her husband to
see what was the matter, and he
began to dance, too, clicking his
fingers as if they were castanets.

And then all the
neighbours, hearing the fuss,
came in too.

Soon everyone in the
village was dancing, kicking up
their heels, twirling, bending
and bowing. They simply could
not stop.

Pablo stepped outside and they followed him, a long line of men and women and children dancing wildly about. And bringing up the rear, danced his stepmother, still carrying the soup kettle. All along the road they went until they danced past the parish church.

Outside the church stood the *cura*, the priest. He was getting a bit of sun and drinking a glass of wine. As soon as the song reached him, he too began to dance, his long robes flapped and billowed about his legs, and the wine glass dropped to the ground, shattering.

Pablo led them from the village and up the mountain road, though the priest cried out for him to stop, and his stepmother begged for mercy. But Pablo did not lift the flute from his lips. He kept on playing.

It is said, in some parts of Granada, that Pablo played his flute until his stepmother begged his pardon, promising never to hurt him again, and then he stopped playing and let everyone go home. But others say that if you listen carefully when you go into the mountains, you can hear him still. Just don't go too close, or you, too, will have to dance.

# Dancing with the Birch Fairy

Once, in a country of birch trees, a girl named Betushka lived with her mother and two goats in a run-down cottage at the foot of a forest. Betushka and her mother were poor and hardworking, but they were merry nonetheless. Never a harsh word passed between them from one week to the next.

As long as the days were fine, Betushka took the goats to pasture in the birch woods. She carried a slice of bread, a wooden cup, an empty spindle and a bundle of flax in her cotton shoulder bag. The bread was for her lunch, and the spindle was for the flaxen thread she spun while watching the goats.

Each morning, her mother would kiss Betushka on the brow. 'Work hard, little daughter,' she always said. 'Keep the goats from harm and fill the spindle before you return.'

Betushka would kiss her mother back, and then skip off, singing a song about goats or spindles or nightingales at day's end. Betushka loved to sing. But even more, she loved to dance.

Now, one fine morning, as Betushka followed the goats into the birch woods, the day seemed especially bright. A song thrush sang its liquid melody from a nearby tree. Betushka waved, kissed her hand, spun around three times and then sat down under the tree. She began to sing back to the bird and unpack her bag. Bread, cup, spindle and flax tumbled into her lap.

Then Betushka pulled fibres from the flax, twirling the spindle so merrily, it hummed over the ground. Lulled by song and spindle, the goats cropped the grass.

When it was midday, with the sun directly overhead, Betushka stopped her work to get water from a nearby stream. Then she sat down again to eat most of the bread, washing it down with the cold stream water. Finally she stood again. Going over to the goats, she gave them each the hard ends of her bread, all the while singing,

*Eat little goats, eat with me,*
*Grow as big as big can be.*

Then she spun around and picked up her skirts, and the goats danced with her.

Suddenly a beautiful woman in a white gossamer gown appeared before Betushka. A wreath of lilies and holly twined in a crown around her head, and her green-gold hair flowed down her back almost to her waist. 'Who are you?' Betushka asked, for women with green-gold hair are rarely seen.

The woman did not answer directly but instead smiled at Betushka, asking in return, 'Betushka, do you like to dance?'

Betushka was astonished. Not only had this glorious creature suddenly appeared, but she knew Betushka's name. And so Betushka lost all her fear. 'Dance? Why I could dance all day long and never tire.'

'Come then,' the woman said, holding out her hand. 'Let me teach you how the birch fairies dance.'

*A birch fairy — of course!* Betushka put her hand in the fairy's. They began to hop and skip, around and around, while all the birds of the forest sang their tunes. Nightingales, greenfinches, and even the thrush that had called to Betushka first, all combined.

Forgetting her goats and her spinning, forgetting all the hard work her mother had asked for, Betushka danced hand in hand with the birch fairy until the last rays of the setting sun lit the clearing. And strange to say, there was no sign underfoot that they had danced all day in the grass.

Suddenly, the birds stopped singing and the birch fairy vanished as mysteriously as she had arrived.

Betushka looked around. There were the goats staring up at her. And there was her spindle, only partly filled with thread.

'Oh,' Betushka said to herself, 'what will mother say? I have danced away the entire day and have hardly any work to show for it.' She put the spindle into her bag and, raising her hand, drove the goats from the wood.

As she walked home, Betushka scolded herself again and again for forgetting her duty. 'I shall never do any such thing again,' she said. 'But oh! The birch fairy was beautiful, and how I love to dance!' Still, she resolved never to be so selfish again.

When at last Betushka reached home, she came into the little cottage without speaking, set down the bag, and sat in the chimney corner on the three-legged stool.

She was so quiet that her mother asked, 'Betushka, my beloved child, what is wrong? You are not singing. You are not dancing. The spindle is only half full. Are you ill?'

Betushka looked up, eyes brimming with tears. 'I am feeling strange, dear mother, that is all.' She said nothing about the birch fairy. 'Tomorrow,' she promised, 'tomorrow I will work twice as hard to make up for today.'

So just at sunrise the next morning, Betushka took the goats up to the birch woods, though this time she did not sing. When she sat down to spin, she worked very hard, for she had every intention of doing twice her usual amount.

At noon, Betushka picked a few strawberries and ate her bread, sharing the crusts with the goats. But this time she did not dance with them. 'Dancing will only take away time from my work,' she told them.

Suddenly, the birch fairy appeared. 'If you will not dance with your goats, at least come and dance with me, Betushka.'

Betushka hung her head, ashamed and — if truth be told — somewhat afraid. 'Please, madam,' she pleaded,

'leave me alone. My mother and I have little enough and I must work. Before sunset, I have to double my spinning, to make up for yesterday.'

The birch fairy laughed, and it was a sound as lovely as the thrush's song. 'If you dance with me today, Betushka, I promise that the spinning will get done.'

'Oh, madam, if only I could believe that,' Betushka said, tears in her eyes.

'Listen to the birds singing. They will tell you that birch fairies never lie.'

As the fairy spoke, the birds in the trees burst into song and Betushka smiled through her tears. A little reluctantly, she held out her hands. The birch fairy took them and, once again, they began to dance, on and on until evening.

As the sun's rays began to desert the little clearing, the birch fairy dropped Betushka's hands. Betushka turned and saw her nearly empty spindle. Once again, she burst into tears.

'You promised. . .' she began. But the birch fairy was already spinning, winding the flax around a small birch tree and spinning it into thread around the spindle. By the time the sun was completely gone, the flax was all spun into a glorious thread.

'Here,' said the birch fairy, 'did I not say that birch fairies never lie? Now remember — do your work but never grumble. Say it after me.'

'Do your work but never grumble,' repeated Betushka obediently.

'Good,' said the fairy, kissing Betushka on the forehead. The kiss burned like fire and ice at the same time. Then the fairy disappeared.

'Thank you! Oh, thank you, birch fairy!' Betushka cried, and drove the goats home, singing as she went. When she reached the little cottage, she handed her mother the full spindle.

'Well, well, I see nothing ails you today,' her mother said. She bent to kiss Betushka on her forehead, but there was a smudge there, like ashes from a fire. She wiped it off with her apron.

'I felt well enough today to sing and dance and spin, too,' Betushka said, but she never mentioned the birch fairy.

The next day, even before sunrise, Betushka gathered the goats and went up to the birch woods. As the goats grazed, Betushka sang and spun, and did not dare to wonder what would happen next.

At noon, the beautiful birch fairy appeared. This time, she took Betushka by the waist.

'Come dance, Betushka,' cried the fairy.

'Promise me a full spindle,' Betushka said.

'I promise you something even better,' said the birch fairy.

'I want the full spindle,' Betushka said, 'for how else can Mother and I live?'

'You must trust me,' said the birch fairy, smiling at her. 'Birch fairies never lie.' And she led Betushka to dance.

The birds in the trees began their music, and Betushka and the fairy spun about and danced until the sun began to set. Then Betushka looked around. Her spindle was only half full, and the fairy did not pick it up to finish the spinning. *Oh no!* Betushka thought, *what shall I tell Mother?*

But instead, the fairy had taken up Betushka's bag, spun around with it three times, then given Betushka back the bag, which now seemed full.

'Do not look in the bag, dear Betushka,' she said, 'not here in the birch woods. But once you are home in your own domain, you may open the bag. Remember — do your work and never grumble.' Then she kissed Betushka again on the forehead, a kiss that burned like fire and ice, and disappeared.

Betushka started home with her goats and the half-full spindle. She waited until she was well away from the birch woods. Then she looked into the bag.

'Oh no!' she said aloud, for all that was inside were birch leaves. Dry birch leaves.

She put her hand in and threw a handful out, angry with the birch fairy, but angrier with herself. Then she stopped. The birch leaves would make fine bedding for her goats at any rate. And she would show the leaves first to her mother, confessing all she had done. Putting the half-spun spindle of flax on top of the leaves in the bag, she trudged on.

When Betushka got home, long after dark, her mother was waiting anxiously at the cottage door.

'What kind of spindle did you bring me yesterday?' her mother asked. 'I wove and wove, but the spindle always remained full. I grumbled to the spindle, "What evil spell is on you?" At that very instant, the thread vanished from the spindle. Tell me what this means.'

*Do your work, but never grumble.* So the fairy had warned Betushka, and she had not told her mother. So now it all spilled out: the bird music, the dance with the fairy and her rewards — some good and some bad.

'A birch fairy!' exclaimed her mother, alarmed. 'That explains it. They dance at midday and at midnight. Lucky for you that you are a polite little girl, Betushka. You are loving and kind. If you had been naughty and mean or impolite — or if you had been a boy — you might not have escaped alive.' Then she added, 'To think that you did not tell me what the fairy said. If I had not grumbled, I still might have a room full of thread.'

She gave her daughter a kiss.

'Never mind. You are safe, and I still got twice as
much woven with that thread than I ever have done before,
so we can thank the fairy for that.'

Then Betushka told her mother about the bag of leaves. She
lifted out the spindle and the unspun flax. 'See, Mother! At least I can
make a new bed for the goats.'

Her mother looked in the bag, clapped her hands, and laughed.
'Look indeed! Oh, thank you, dear birch fairy.'

Betushka looked as well. The birch leaves had turned to gold.

'Oh, Mother, I have done you wrong. The fairy warned me not
to open the bag until I got home, but I did. And I grumbled and
threw out some of the leaves. We might have been rich indeed.'

'Never mind, my darling child,' her mother said. 'You might have emptied the entire bag. You did not, and for that we must remain grateful. Besides, there is a fortune here — more than enough for us — and some left over to give to the poor.'

And that is what they did. With the birch fairy's gift, they bought a small farm with a garden and some cows. They hired a goat boy. And they put a great deal of money into the poor box in church.

Though Betushka often went back to the birch woods looking for the fairy, she never saw her again. But Betushka was careful to always leave a bowl of fresh milk and a blessing. Just in case.

# When the Goddess Danced

In ancient Egypt, Ra, god of the sun, father of all creation, looked down upon the land, the green of the Nile river valley and the red of the desert. Ra was all-powerful and, being a god, he could behave in ways that mortals could not.

Ra used to visit earth as an invisible being and there, in one of the cities, he spied Ruditdidit, wife of his priest, Rausir. Ruditdidit was a great beauty. Her hair was dark and straight, her big eyes were lined with kohl. Ra fell instantly in love with her.

Now Ra was often in love and he wooed Ruditdidit passionately, becoming visible only to her. No mortal could resist him. Soon Ruditdidit became pregnant with triplets.

The god did everything he could to make sure Ruditdidit had an easy time. He sent her figs, grapes and pomegranates. He sent her earthenware jars of goat milk. He made the sun shine brightly and the Nile River whisper lullabies in her ears.

For nine months, Ruditdidit did no work, waiting for the birth of her three babies. But when it was time for her labour, her pains were terrible. She wept, she cried, she called out to great Ra for help.

He looked down at her from the heavens and then called four goddesses to him. They were Isis who was goddess of rebirth and teacher of women; Nephthys, goddess of death; and the helpers Maskhonuit and Hiquit. He called as well

Khnum, god of the source of the Nile. The five bowed to Ra, and did as he wished, riding to earth in his sun-chariot.

But these gods could not just arrive at a priest's house as themselves. Ra had warned them that they must go in disguise, and not let the priest Rausir know who they were. So three of the goddesses came dressed as street musicians. The fourth, Isis, draped herself in gold jewellery and carried round wooden clappers. Anyone who saw her would take her at once for a dancer. As for Khnum, he pretended to be their porter and carried their instruments — the lute, the lyre and the drum.

Thus disguised, the five were allowed in the priest's mud-brick house, for in those days street dancers were also known to be fine midwives. In fact, Rausir was delighted to see them, for his wife's cries had not ceased for twenty-four hours, and he was afraid she might die and the children with her.

'Welcome, welcome,' he told the dancer and the musicians, leading them immediately to the room where his wife lay.

Now though Rausir the priest did not recognise the gods in their disguises, Ruditdidit did, for she carried three half-immortals in her womb. She stopped her moaning for a moment, sat up, and clapped her hands. Even after a whole day and night of weeping, she was still beautiful.

'Oh, sing for me,' she cried. 'Dance for me.'

And they did.

Nephthys strummed the lute, Maskhonuit the lyre, and Hiquit picked up the drum and began pounding on it, supplying a perfect rhythm for dancing.

Being a male, Khnum stayed outside the chamber and drank barley beer with the priest. They ate bread and figs and spoke of the Nile. Anything but Ruditdidit's labour, for it was not right for men to speak of it.

But in Ruditdidit's chamber, with the music playing, Isis started to dance. She carried a short wooden stick in her hand, its top a carved gazelle head. Her bare feet carried her around the room, hips swaying. Coming near the bed, she placed the cane by Ruditdidit's right hand. Then she twirled and stamped upon the ground, the clappers on her fingers keeping rhythm with the musicians.

Now Isis reached down to Ruditdidit on her bed, pulling the moaning woman to her feet.

'Come, sister, dance,' Isis told her, and began twirling her around the room, faster and faster. She made Ruditdidit's stomach ripple like waves, her hips like mountains shuddering in a quake.

Ruditdidit did as Isis commanded, her belly moving back and forth, up and down until she was quite dizzy but the pain had receded.

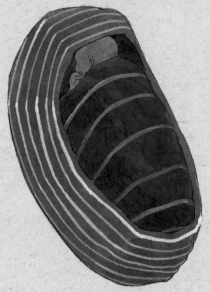

Then, when Ruditdidit was ready for the birth, Isis stopped dancing. She led Ruditdidit back to her bed where the woman squatted by the bedside and began to push. Isis put her hands out, and the triplets fell into them — one, two, three. As she caught the infants, she handed each one to her sister goddesses, who had put down their instruments to receive the children. One, two, three fine boys.

'One day,' Isis told Ruditdidit, 'your sons shall rule Egypt. But now you all must rest.'

Ruditdidit lay down on the bed, and Isis placed the three babies around her. Then, dancing once again, Isis left the room and called to Rausir, 'Your children await you.'

The priest left a basket of corn as payment and ran in to see his wife. Isis flipped the basket into the air. When it came down, it struck the ground and turned into a basket of gold coins.

But the priest Rausir did not find that out until much, much later, for three new babies and a tired wife turned out to be a lot of work.

# Tam O'Shanter

In the town of Alloway, in Ayrshire, the old church — or *kirk* as the Scots call it — had stood for two hundred years before its congregation deserted it for a newer one. Left to the depredations of wind and rain, the roof of the kirk fell in, and the walls tumbled partway down.

And after a while, word got out that the place was haunted.

No one went near it after dark.

No one dared.

Now it was on a market day, in the nearby town of Ayr, that a young farmer, Tam O'Shanter, rode home rather too late. He'd stayed after the fair's close, talking and laughing with his friends, and had paid no attention to the time. Suddenly noticing it was getting dark, he worried that his wife would wonder about him and that his horse would be too tired to make the trip back. But he could not stay the night. So, with a fearful heart, he started for home when the dark was already deeper than the light.

He was making his way
towards the old bridge that
crossed the River Doon, which
meant he had to pass by the
very gate of the Alloway kirkyard.
Wouldn't you know it, but he
got there just at the wizard
hour, that time of night when
the world balances between dark
and dawn.

What should he see but a
blaze of light streaming from
the kirk. It was quite odd, since
the kirk was supposed to have
been empty.

'What to do? What to do?'
Tam muttered to himself while
wringing his hands. Fear had
awakened some courage in him.
What to do? What to do? The
old folks say that running from
haunts is as bad as running
towards them. But Tam had
forgotten that part of the
wisdom. As if half enchanted,
he got off his horse and
decided to see what was
going on.

When he reached
the gate, he could look right
through the ribs and arches of the

big Gothic window that still faced the highway. He could scarcely believe it! There was a troop of old witches merrily dancing around their master, who was keeping them going with the power of his great bagpipes. They were hopping and reeling and crying out with delight as if they were youngsters. Faster and faster they went about, clicking their fingers, lifting their skirts, flinging their legs about and twirling.

Tam led his horse right up to the window where silently he watched all the goings-on.

It seemed to him that he could make out the faces of many old women of the neighbourhood. Why, there was Mistress McDonald, the butcher's widow, and there was old Lady Carrick. And an alewife he knew only as Janet. And many others. They were dressed in their *sarks* — their smocks — not in black dresses like the witches in stories. Their tartan sashes were hung over their right shoulders and down to their waists.

What a grand time they seemed to be having, dancing the Eightsome Reel, clicking their fingers and crying out to one another, 'Ho there!' and 'Well done!' Next, they danced the Highland Fling, hands above their heads, kicking their feet up in the air. Then on they went to Strip the Willow with four couples trading places over and over again. And then they began the Dashing White Sergeant, in a great circle, eight steps to the left and then eight steps back again.

Tam watched further, his heart beating wildly, as the witches danced strathspeys and jigs and a dozen more reels, all without stopping in between. He found himself tapping out the time on his chest, and his right foot marked the music as well. He was almost tempted to join in. But he stopped himself in time. If the witches noticed him at all, he would be in trouble for certain. So he kept his feet from dancing.

As he stood watching, enjoying the music and the dance but not daring to participate, he noticed one witch, a handsome younger woman, whose smock was considerably shorter than the rest — a cutty sark. When she leapt and twirled, Tam was so tickled that he involuntarily burst out, with a loud laugh, calling, 'Good leap, Maggie with the cutty sark!'

At the sound of Tam's voice, the pipes groaned to a stop. The master's face turned dark and full of anger. He glanced around, growling like some awful beast. The witches all looked up as well, and one pointed out Tam at the window.

*Now I'm in for it!* Tam thought, courage leaving
him. For surely the witches would kill him. He let out a groan
louder than the pipes. Then he turned and leapt back on his horse.
Yanking its head around, he spurred it away at top speed. He knew
he had to make it to the bridge before the witches could catch him.
Once in the middle of the stream, no diabolical power in the world
could touch him because everyone knew magic could not cross
running water.

The horse was as frightened as Tam, for behind and above them rode the witches on their brooms, screaming and cackling and crying for Tam's head or heart, or whichever part of him they could get to first. So, rolling its eyes up in fear, the poor horse kept galloping towards the bridge, and Tam kept kicking its sides with his heels, yelling to it, 'Faster, for the Good Lord's sake, faster!' And the witches kept screaming for Tam's blood. Oh, but it was a wild ride!

And then the bridge was in sight and Tam thought for a minute that they might actually make it. The horse's hooves clopped onto the bridge, and they'd all but reached the middle, when one of the pursuing hags jumped off her broom and caught the poor horse's tail in her hand.

'Got ya!'

The horse reared and then leapt forwards. Its tail, as if blasted by a stroke of lightning, gave way, and horse and rider clattered to the middle of the bridge.

The old witch screamed out, 'I'll have you yet, manling,' and she ran after them.

But Tam and the horse were now over the middle of the bridge, and the witch could not pass further. 'Curse you!' she cried as they galloped beyond her reach.

They raced all the way home, the sound of the old witch's curses echoing in their ears.

What Tam told his wife to explain away his horse's docked tail, no one knows. But that tail never grew back. To its last hours — many years later — the horse served as an awful warning to any of the farmers of the neighbourhood not to stay too late in Ayr market after the close of the fair.

As for the old kirk in Alloway — why, the ruins are still there, should you wish to visit. Only be sure to do it in daylight and not at the wizard hour.

# The Little Bird Who Went Dancing

The *griot*, the village storyteller, told me this story, and so I tell it to you.

There was a girl, a beautiful girl, the daughter of a praise singer, and her name was Tiyoro. She loved to dance.

Now one day, a handsome young man named Lawali saw her at a dance and he fell in love with beautiful Tiyoro. He went up to her and said, his hand on his heart, 'Tiyoro, love me or hate me, accept me or refuse me, take me or leave me, I will still love you forever.'

She turned her back on him. 'I am sorry, but I do not love you.'

He smiled at her back. 'I will go and speak to your mother.'

Tiyoro shrugged and kept on dancing.

So, Lawali went to Tiyoro's mother. 'I love beautiful Tiyoro,' he said to her.

Tiyoro's mother smiled. 'If she loves you, that is good. What do I have to do with it anyway?'

But when he went back to the dance and told Tiyoro what her mother had said, beautiful Tiyoro only answered,

'I am sorry, but I do not love you.'

And she kept on dancing.

Well, Lawali begged and pleaded, but he got nowhere. So at last he went to a magician. And the magician said, 'How much do you love beautiful Tiyoro?'

'I love her as long as the Niger River flows,' Lawali said.

'That is long indeed,' said the magician. And he turned Lawali
into a magnificent little bird with bright feathers.
    Now the beautiful Tiyoro had forgotten all about the
young man who had spoken to her at the dance. And that very
day, she was down by the riverside with her sister, and they
were washing clothes. Suddenly a magnificent little
bird with bright feathers flew down and
sat on the clean clothes.

'Oh, oh!' Tiyoro cried. 'That is the most magnificent bird
I have ever seen. I love it.' As she reached over for it, the bird gave
a little chirrup and flew to her hand.
    'Oh, oh!' Tiyoro cried out again. 'I love this little bird.' And,
forgetting the clean clothes, she took the bird back to her mother.

'Mother, this is to be my bird and no one else's,' said Tiyoro. 'See how he sits in my hand.'

Her mother stared at the bird and shrugged. 'If you love it, that is good. What do I have to do with it anyway?'

Well, that evening, there was to be another dance, and how Tiyoro loved dancing. So she wanted to go to the village. She dressed in her best clothes and put on her best cowrie shell necklace. She was about to leave when the bird spoke to her.

'Chirrup. Do not leave me here. Take me with you, or take me back to the river where you found me.'

Tiyoro turned to her mother. 'Did you hear that? The bird spoke to me and asked to go to the dance.'

Her mother stared at the bird and shrugged. 'If you love it, take it to the dance. Otherwise, let it go free. What do I have to do with it anyway?'

Well, Tiyoro didn't want to let the bird go, so she picked it up and put it on her shoulder, and off she and her sister went to the dance.

When they got to the village square where the dance was to be held, Tiyoro tried to put the bird down on a branch.

'Chirrup,' sang the bird. 'Oh no, Tiyoro, I want to dance with you.'

Tiyoro turned to her sister. 'Did you hear that? The bird spoke to me and said he wants to dance with me.'

Her sister stared at the bird and shrugged. 'If you love it, take it in your hand and dance. Otherwise, let it go free. What do I have to do with it anyway?'

Well, Tiyoro didn't want to let the bird go, so she took it in her hand and began to dance and dance. They danced until the night grew dark and stars dotted the sky. They danced until the first rays of sun touched the Niger River.

And everyone said, 'Could Tiyoro not find a person to dance with? Could she only find a bird?'

Well, that stung Tiyoro's pride, and when they got home, she tried to leave the bird outside. But when she lay down to sleep, the little bird flew outside the window and sang:

> *Tiyoro, let me sit on the windowsill.*
> *I'll keep watch beside you.*
> *I will see you're safe from harm,*
> *Let nothing bad betide you.*

'Mother,' Tiyoro cried out, 'what should I do?'

'It is only a bird,' said her mother. 'What harm can befall you? Besides, what do I have to do with it anyway?'

So Tiyoro let the bird in and it sat on the windowsill while she got in under the covers. Then it sang:

> *Tiyoro, let me sit upon the chair,*
> *Let me sit beside you.*
> *I will keep you safe from harm,*
> *Let nothing bad betide you.*

'Sister,' Tiyoro cried out, 'what should I do?'

'It is only a bird,' said her sister. 'What harm can befall you? Besides, what do I have to do with it anyway?'

So beautiful Tiyoro let the little bird sit on the chair by her bed. Then she snuggled down and fell asleep.

When she woke in the morning, it was not a little bird that slept in the chair. He had turned into a handsome young man. So they were married.

At least that is what the griot told me. So I have told you.

# Waltz

## *from* The Twelve Dancing Princesses

### The Dance

The basic step pattern for the waltz is: step, slide to the side, close, with each step corresponding to a single beat of music. The emphasis is placed on the first beat, giving a rhythm of ONE-two-three to the dance. It is customary for the man to lead and the woman to follow, performing the same moves as the man but stepping backwards.

### The Costume

Important to the waltz were the long, elegant ballgowns that the women used to wear, with flat silk or soft leather shoes that could easily be worn through by dancing all night. Men wore tails to complement the women's beautiful dresses.

### Learning the Waltz

Step 1: Leader: start by taking a long stride forwards onto your left foot.
Follower: your first step will be backwards onto your right foot.

Step 2: Leader: move your right foot diagonally to the top-right corner of an imaginary rectangle on the floor and lift up onto your toes.
Follower: you will move your left foot in the same direction.

Step 3: Leader: finally, bring your left foot beside your right foot and lower your toes and then your heels as your feet come together.
Follower: you will bring your right foot beside your left foot.

Step 4: Repeat this sequence, starting on the right foot. As you move, turn slightly in one direction each time so that you travel around the floor in a circle.

# Noh Dancing
## *from* Robe of Feathers

### The Dance

Dances in a Noh drama are usually performed solo. The dancers keep their feet in close contact with the floor, so that they seem to glide across the stage, expressing deep emotions through very slight movements of the body. Their goal is to express the essence of the story as powerfully as possible. When they succeed, members of the audience cry out in appreciation.

### The Costume

The actors, who are all male, wear full-length, richly coloured, elaborate robes of silk. A notable aspect of any Noh performance is the exquisitely carved wooden masks that are worn when the lead actor is playing an old man, a youth, a woman or a spirit.

### Watching Noh

Noh's understated dance patterns and gestures, which are called *kata*, are highly symbolic and have not changed for centuries. One form of kata is *shiori*, an imitation of weeping in which a hand and sleeve are raised to the eyes. A way in which actors show excitement is through *yuken*, in which an open fan is raised in one hand and lowered at the level of the heart. To show greater excitement, or *ryo-yuken*, the fan is held with both hands.

# Limbo

## *from* Making the Stone Smoke

### The Dance

Today's limbo — accompanied by calypso and steel drum music — is a laid-back style of dance. During the dance, two people hold the limbo stick as another person attempts to shuffle underneath. Dancers take turns going under the pole while bending over backwards. They need an excellent sense of balance and strong back and leg muscles to be able to shuffle under easily. Good dancers can sometimes go as low as seven inches from the ground!

### The Costume

The limbo is performed in laid-back costumes to reflect the nature of the dance. People tend to wear light clothing with their bellies exposed to make it as easy as possible to pass below the limbo stick.

### Learning the Limbo

Step 1: Two people hold the limbo stick.

Step 2: The first dancer moves underneath the stick by arching backwards.

Step 3: After each dancer has had a turn, the stick is lowered and the dancers bend back to shuffle underneath it again. If at any point, a dancer touches the stick or the ground, he or she is 'out'. The dance continues until only one dancer remains.

# Flamenco

## from The Shepherd's Flute

### The Dance

There are many different moves in flamenco dancing. The male dancers' steps include a great deal of intricate footwork (*zapateado*) and heel tapping (*taconeo*), whereas female dancers rely more on expressive movements of the hands and fingers (*florea*), arms (*braceo*) and upper torso.

### The Costume

Flamenco dancing is characterised by the bright, often multi-frilled dresses worn by the women, which originate from the work dresses worn by nineteenth-century Andalusian women. Special shoes are also worn — high-heeled yet sturdy and with tiny nails at the heel and toe to make a tapping sound. Men typically wear suits with high-waisted trousers and a short jacket.

### Learning the Flamenco

Step 1: Ladies, grab your skirt with your left hand. Men, put your hands on either side of your hips while bending your elbows.

Step 2: Ladies, raise your left knee while you raise your skirt. Men, do a hop-step-stomp on your right foot, then do the same with your left foot.

Step 3: Ladies, raise your right hand high up in the air, and stamp your left foot on the ground, then stamp your right foot. Still holding onto your skirt, keep stamping with your hand held high, and slowly move around in a circle. Men, move your arms in a styled fashion — using *duende* — and stomp while twisting your body, flowing to the beat of the music.

# Polka

## *from* Dancing with the Birch Fairy

### The Dance

The polka begins with couples either facing each other or side by side, with the man's arm around the woman's waist, and her arm on his shoulder. There is no strict formation to the dance, and couples may glide across the floor in any direction they wish — but they must be careful not to run into other dancers!

### The Costume

In Czechoslovakia (now the Czech Republic), female polka dancers traditionally wore a white, puffy-sleeved blouse with a waistcoat, flouncy skirt and — like the birch fairy in the story — a wreath of flowers around their heads. The male costume included a white shirt, white trousers, leather dancing boots and a sleeveless jacket.

### Learning the Polka

Step 1: Start with a preliminary hop on your right foot, and step forwards on your left foot.

Step 2: Bring the right foot to the left, putting weight on your right foot, and step again on the left foot. Hold this for one beat, keeping your weight on the left foot.

Step 3: Repeat this series of steps again, but starting with the opposite foot — using the left foot for the hop and your right foot as the one that steps forwards. If you are dancing facing your partner, then the person following steps backwards instead of forwards, with the right foot for Step 1 and the left foot for Step 3.

# Belly Dancing
## *from* When the Goddess Danced

### The Dance

In belly dancing, hips shimmy up and down, the stomach undulates and the arms move in snake-like patterns. The main emphasis is on the hips, and common moves include circles, loops, figures of eight, lifts and drops. For example, a horizontal hip circle may be done by keeping your body still while you slide your hips to one side, forwards, to the other side, and then back.

### The Costume

Traditional costumes vary from a simple fitted top, a hip belt and a skirt to elaborate beaded outfits. A scarf or piece of fabric held in the dancer's hand may also be used in part of the dance to accompany the movements of the belly and hips.

### Learning the Belly Dance

Step 1: Keep your knees bent and your feet hip-width apart. Raise your arms.

Step 2: Push your right hip to the side, leaning onto your right leg.

Step 3: Push your left hip to the side, leaning onto your left leg. Repeat both moves as much as you like, varying the speed at which you sway from side to side.

# Scottish Reels

## *from* Tam O'Shanter

### The Dance

Scottish dancing has many different variations: the Hamilton House, which is a jig-time reel for three couples; the Duke of Perth, danced by three couples in two lines; the Foursome Reel, which is also known by the name Reel and Strathspey; and the Eightsome Reel that is danced by four couples in a circle. Reeling is still very popular in Scotland, at social events such as parties and weddings. Forms of the reel are also performed throughout Britain at ceilidhs or barn dances.

### The Costume

Men traditionally wear kilts or tartan trousers. Women wear ballgowns with tartan sashes over the shoulder.

### Learning Scottish Reels

Each of the Scottish reels has its own sequence of steps, turns and spins, danced with a partner. However, all reels are danced to the same basic step:

Step 1: Put your hands on your hips.

Step 2: Do a quick hop-skip-hop step to the right, putting your weight first onto your right foot, then your left foot, then your right again.

Step 3: Repeat this step to the left. This is called 'setting'.

Use this same three-beat step when you are moving forwards or around in a circle — your stride in this case will be long-short-short.

# Malian Dance

## *from* The Little Bird Who Went Dancing

### The Dance

In Mali, the Dogon people are famous for their funeral masquerades, special ceremonies in which the souls of the dead are led to their final resting place. The masks are meant to hide the individual dancers (all men), making them anonymous and giving the impression that it is the spirit, not the person, that is dancing. The masks are made in secret for a particular occasion. There are over eighty varieties of mask, the most famous being the *kanaga*, resembling a bird of prey with outstretched wings.

### The Costume

Dancers cover themselves in costumes of grasses and fibres. Beads, shells or leather and metal attachments are often added depending on the character represented by the dancer.

### Watching Malian Dance

In a typical funeral dance, the dancers wear masks with small models of people on the top to represent people that have died. The dancer bends over, touches the earth with the models and lifts his body upwards in a gesture that allows the spirits of the dead to move from earth to heaven.

 # Bibliography

## General

Cohen, Selma Jeanne (ed.), *International Encyclopaedia of Dance*, Oxford University Press, New York, 2004

Grau, Andree, *Dance*, Dorling Kindersley, London, 2003; New York, 2005

Jonas, Gerald, *Dancing*, BBC Books, London: 1992; Harry N. Abrams, New York, 1998

Leach, Maria, ed., *Funk & Wagnall's Standard Dictionary of Folklore, Mythology, and Legend*, Funk & Wagnalls, New York, 1959

## The Twelve Dancing Princesses

Bottomer, Paul, *Waltz* (Dance Club Series), Southwater, London, 2003

Grimm, Jacob and Wilhelm, *The Brothers Grimm: Popular Tales*, Brian Alderson, trans., Victor Gollancz, London, 1978

Grimm, Jacob and Wilhelm, *Household Tales*, Margaret Hunt, trans., George Bell, London, 1884

Singleton, Esther, *The Goldenrod Fairy Book*, Dodd, Mead & Company, New York, 1903

Thompson, Stith, *The Folktale*, University of California Press, Berkeley, 1977

www.bobjanuary.com/waltz.htm

www.centralhome.com/ballroomcountry/waltz.htm

www.surlalunefairytales.com/twelvedancing/notes.html

## Robe of Feathers

Komparu, Nobutaka, *Takigi Noh*, Graphic-Sha Publishing Co. Ltd, Tokyo, 1987

www.artelino.com/articles/noh_theater.asp

concise.britannica.com/ebc/article?tocId=9358235

etext.lib.virginia.edu/japanese/noh/intro.html

linus.socs.uts.edu.au/~don/pubs/noh.html

members.jcom.home.ne.jp/fujinone/e_hakuryo.htm

www.japan-guide.com/list/e1000.html

www.op97.org/cyberteen/2004/spring/masks/

www.sacred-texts.com/shi/npj/npj31.htm

## Making the Stone Smoke

Abrahams, Roger, *Afro-American Folktales: Stories from Black Traditions in the New World*, Pantheon Books, New York, 1985

www.infoplease.com/ce6/world/A0851931.html

www.svgtourism.com/channels/1.asp?id=60

www.theatredance.com/mhist01.html

## The Shepherd's Flute

Armstrong, Lucile, *Dances of Spain. I: South, Centre and North-West*, Max Parrish & Company, London, 1950

Armstrong, Lucile, *Dances of Spain. II: North-East and East*, Max Parrish & Company, London, 1950

Boggs, Ralph Steele & Davis, Mary Gould, *Three Golden Oranges & Other Spanish Folk Tales*, Longmans, Green & Co., New York, 1936

Mitchell, Timothy, *Flamenco Deep Song*, Yale University Press, Rhode Island, 1994

Pohren, D. E., *Lives and Legends of Flamenco: A Biographical History*, Society of Spanish Studies, Madrid, 1964

Pohren, D. E., *The Art of Flamenco*, Society of Spanish Studies, Madrid, 1972

Serrano, Juan & Jose Elgorraga, *Flamenco, Body and Soul: An Aficionado's Introduction*, University of Califorina Press at Fresno, 1990

*Flamenco* (film, 1995), directed by Carlos Saura

www.red2000.com/spain/flamenco

## Dancing with the Birch Fairy

Briggs, Katharine, *An Encyclopedia of Fairies: Hobgoblins, Brownies, Bogies, and Other Supernatural Creatures*, Pantheon Books, New York, 1976

Fillmore, Parker, *Czechoslovak Fairy Tales*, The Quinn & Boden Company, New Jersey, 1919

Frazer, Sir James, *The Golden Bough*, Worsdsworth Editions, Hertfordshire, 1993

Haviland, Virginia, *Favorite Fairy Tales Told in Czechoslovakia*, "The Wood Fairy," Little Brown, Boston, 1959

Helfman, Elizabeth, *Maypoles and Wood Demons, The Meaning of Trees*, Seabury Press, New York, 1972

Pellowski, Anne, *Hidden Stories in Plants*, "The Wild Woman of the Birch Wood," Macmillan, New York, 1990

www.britannica.com/eb/article?eu=62217&hook=241579

www.centralhome.com/ballroomcountry/polka.htm

www.mothergoddess.com/other.htm

www.treesforlife.org.uk/forest/mythfolk/birch.html

www.usc.edu/dept/polish_music/dance/polka.html

## When the Goddess Danced

Buonaventura, Wendy, *Serpent of the Nile*, Interlink Books, New York, 1998

Stewart, Iris J., *Sacred Woman, Sacred Dance: Awakening Spirituality through Dance and Ritual*, Inner Traditions, Rochester, VT, 2000

www.bellydance.org/articles/what_is_bellydance.html

www.bdancer.com

www.learn-to-belly-dance.com/styles.html

www.middleeasterndance.homestead.com

www.shira.net

www.zehara.co.uk/bellydancefacts.htm

## Tam O'Shanter

Emmerson, George S., *A Social History of Scottish Dance*, McGill-Queen's University Press, Montreal, Canada, 1972

Emmerson, George S., *Scotland through Her Country Dances*, Johnson Publications, London, 1967.

Farmer, H. G., *A History of Music in Scotland*, Hinrichsen, London, 1947

Furgusson, J. Delancey, ed., *Robert Burns' Letters*, Oxford University Press, Oxford, 1931

Johnson, David, *Music and Society in Lowland Scotland in the Eighteenth Century*, Oxford University Press, Oxford, 1972

Robbins, Rossell Hope, *The Encyclopedia of Witchcraft and Demonology*, Crown Publishers, New York, 1959

www.burnsheritagepark.com/archive_news.php?story=37

www.mysteriousbritain.co.uk/Scotland/ayrshire/ayrshire2.html

www.rabbie-burns.com/the_poems/tamoshanter.cfm.html

www.robertburns.org/encyclopedia

www.standingstones.com/scotdanc.html

www.streetswing.com

## The Little Bird Who Went Dancing

Dagan, Esther A., ed., *The Spirit's Dance in Africa: Evolution, Transformation and Continuity in Sub-Sahara*, Galerie Amarad African Arts Publications, Canada, 1997

Dorson, Richard M., ed., *African Folklore*, Indiana University Press, Indiana, 1972

www.geographia.com/mali/

tcd.freehosting.net/djembemande/jelicds.html

www.africaguide.com/country/mali/culture.htm

www.hamillgallery.com/DOGON/DogonMasks/DogonMasks.html

www.princetonol.com/groups/iad/lessons/middle/afrilink.htm